# FATAL PERCEPTION

# BOOKS BY REBECCA HEMLOCK

## An Arctic Mystery series
*Bitter Betrayal*
*Deadly Decisions*

## Granton house Mysteries Series
*The Secret of the 14th Room*
*The Secret Diary of Deadly Deception*
*Hidden Passages to Dark Secrets*

## Oakwood Springs PD Series
*Fury in the Shadows*
*Fatal Perception*

Paperback ISBN: 979-8-9885518-9-8
E-book ISBN: 978-1-7368452-9-5



Bluecap Publishing
Ashland, KY 41102
bluecapbooks@gmail.com

*"Therefore I say unto you, Take no thought for your life, what ye shall eat, or what ye shall drink; nor yet for your body, what ye shall put on. Is not the life more than meat, and the body than raiment?*

*Behold the fowls of the air: for they sow not, neither do they reap, nor gather into barns; yet your heavenly Father feedeth them. Are ye not much better than they?"*

## *Mathew 6:25-26 (KJV)*

# FATAL PERCEPTION

REBECCA HEMLOCK

# CHAPTER 1

Megan Holmes gripped her car keys as if she wanted to grab onto something solid, anything that might keep her from the ocean of tears that threatened to sweep through her. She was out of breath just from keeping them down; she could almost taste the saltiness as they pooled up in her throat. Maryann Baker completely humiliated her today. It wasn't the first time or the hundredth, but it was the straw that broke the camel's back.

She pulled her Toyota Camry into the familiar, secluded parking lot, already feeling two big tears welling up. She took a deep breath and clenched her jaw tightly, determined to keep it together. Taking a deep breath, she grabbed her handbag and stepped out of the car, using her free hand to firmly shut the door, as if it created a barricade trapping the tormenting thoughts of Maryann inside. If only it worked that way.

The Ohio River breeze carried hints of earthy coolness. It usually offered comfort, as if the wind carried more than smells and bits of nature floating in it. Not today though. Still, she paused for a moment to savor it, dragging the crisp air deeply into her lungs, allowing it to push her forward up the gravel path.

With each footstep, Megan reminded herself that running away from bullies didn't make her a coward. Her tears, however, made her question that logic. Maryann had tried to push her around for a few years now, and Megan managed to fight back without losing her integrity. But this time was different. She nearly lost her cool right there in the middle of the church sanctuary.

She kept her gaze on the gravel path that led into the woods. Each step crunching under her ballerina flats was usually a welcomed sound, but today it made her want to grimace. Time alone would be the best thing for her right now. There was a lot of praying to do. Should she continue working as a Journalist for the Oakwood Springs paper, if this was the kind of treatment, she'd receive? She wanted the answer to be no after the day she had. But if she was going to continue to work for them, she would do the job right. No matter who it affected.

For a moment, her imagination transported her back to the inside of the Oakwood Springs Community Church. Maryann's angry expression and tight lips appeared in her head. Her boney finger was in Meg's face, nearly touching her nose.

The phrase, "I'll make sure you regret this," repeated in her mind like a drumbeat. Ever since her husband became a city council member of Oakwood Springs, Maryann walked around with her head held high as if she'd just become queen of the small town. Trying to shake off the menacing words, Meg forced herself to think about something else.

As she turned the corner, a gravel path stretched out before her, winding through tall grass and wildflowers until it reached a sprawling field. Sitting perched at its edge was the Arbutus House, a gray stone beauty with ivy vines creeping its way around every window, precisely as her parents had designed it. Every summer they set to work restoring the old structure, and she could still picture their familiar silhouettes working through the night beneath a midnight sky. It was there that she learned to tackle her fears; to face them head-on, strengthened by the echo of laughter that bounced off the walls from days gone by.

This was her safe haven and had been since she was six years old. There were three storage sheds behind the main house, and her parents had built a visitor center just off to the side. She didn't have many memories of the condition of the Arbutus House when her parents first bought it. She just remembered that she, her brother and sister would spend a lot of time in the spare bedroom on the second floor their parents used for a storage room. The boxes of relics and supplies that lined the walls made perfect building blocks for a fort. Their own little fortress of solitude. That was where she headed after letting herself in. The seclusion that room offered was just what she needed after today.

The old wooden door latched shut behind her as she made her way across the room. There was a beanbag chair in the corner she used during the days she spent working here with her parents. But today, she let herself drop to the hard wooden floor. It seemed more fitting for some reason. Now she could do it. The tears could freely fall. Why did everyone treat her like a villain or a tattle tale for doing her job?

With a strangled sob, she pulled a small notebook she'd wedged underneath her arm. She desperately tried to keep it dry by wiping the tears off the page. But that hardly mattered. Smudges were already forming on what was supposed to be the draft of her next article. The ink bled in all directions forming lines like a map, as if it couldn't handle the weight of her despair.

As she gasped for breath between sobs, the dim light flickered above her head, casting dancing shadows across the wet paper. She'd never felt so alone. Should she even write this article? Maybe this was God's way of telling her she shouldn't. Across the top of the page, she'd scribbled the words,

**DRUG AND WEAPON SMUGGLING IN OAKWOOD SPRINGS: ARE WE PART OF THE PROBLEM?**

There were a lot of reasons why that title was perfect for this story, but now she was having second thoughts. Who would come for her this time?

Meg allowed her neck to release its tension, leaning her head back. The second her head touched the wall, something stabbed into the left side of her neck. She jolted upright and ran her hand over the old yellow wallpaper, smoothing down the bubbling areas to find the culprit. The paper made a crinkling sound under her hand. She squinted in the dim light to see what poked her.

Her hand stopped on a knot. As she stared at it, she noticed that it was protruding out from the wall. How did she miss that? A loose nail, maybe? The paper in that spot had been torn. She'd been in this room a million times and knew every inch of it. This wasn't here before.

Gripping the wallpaper with the tip of her fingernail, she peeled it back to see what was causing the huge knot.

Someone cut a hole about the size of an apple into the wall and tried to shove the piece back into place. Why would anyone do that? Who could've done this?

She pulled her phone out and quickly found her mom's number, she tapped the number on the small screen then placed it to her ear.

"Meg, are you alright?" Her mom's voice instantly said. Oh yeah. Her parents had been present when Maryann gave her the tongue whipping.

"Yeah. I'm up in the storeroom of the Arbutus house. Did you cut a hole in the wall?"

"Someone cut a hole in the wall!?" Her mom burst out. Guess that answers part of her question. Some rustling sounds came through the phone, then she heard her mom ask her dad if he knew anything about it. The anger in her voice said that someone was really going to get it for this.

"Dad doesn't know either. Did we have a break-in or something?"

"I don't think so. The door was locked when I got here. But why would someone break in to cut a hole in the upstairs wall?" She stared at the hole for a moment, trying to figure out a reason for it. It was big enough to get a decent look at the field in front of the house without having to close one eye. She peered through it. The tree line on the other side of the field came into view.

The wind whipped the trees back and forth, making them look like they were flashing every shade of green at her. The tall grass made a perfect border along where the field turned into forest. She scanned the property as much as she could, until something bizarre caught her attention. She stuck her face up to the hole. A tall, dark figure stood looming. Her head jerked back. There wasn't supposed to be anyone out here today. She peered through the hole a second time. Now the figure was moving through the woods....quickly.

For a moment, her mind went to all the ghost stories that surrounded the Arbutus house. The supposed sightings of glowing Civil War soldiers marching onto the battlefield and standing at attention, as if awaiting orders. She immediately pushed the notion out of her mind. Growing up here, she'd not once spotted anything lurking in the shadows... until today.

*Get a grip!* Was she seriously entertaining the idea of a ghost? This was probably a hunter who wandered onto their property accidentally or a trespasser. More likely a trespasser. Anger twisted in her stomach. Why couldn't people think about what they do and who their actions might affect? She shoved the little piece of the wall back into place.

As she dialed the Oakwood Springs PD, she made her way back to the car to grab her handgun. Hopefully, the situation wouldn't call for her to use it.

Once back outside, the figure stopped for a few seconds, then started moving again. If she hurried, she could see who was out there before they disappeared. She had to know who it was. Friendly or not, they would know better than to trespass here again when the park was closed.

*****

Kyle kept his gaze locked on the ground, scanning for anything that didn't belong there. He'd been doing this for about two hours now and his head was throbbing from staring for so long. These woods was the one place Daniel Carroll was known to frequent. He'd been missing for around twenty four hours and there had been no good leads. Kyle wasn't sure how far he walked. It was easy to get turned around in here. The thick vines made a blanket that covered the forest floor and most of the tree trunks. The worn paths here and there, were the only places where the ground was visible.

He stopped for a moment and closed his eyes, pinching the bridge of his nose to relieve his headache, which was getting stronger by the minute. He checked his surroundings, looking for something unique that would help him remember which way he'd was going.

Straight ahead was a clearing where some trees had been cut down, allowing sunlight into the shadowy woods. In the center of the brightly lit spot stood a stone structure. He squinted, trying to see it better, but it was far away enough for some vine covered trees to obstruct part of his view.

Maybe that's where Carroll went. It was the first promising clue he'd found since coming out here. Why these husbands never thought to tell their wives what they were up to, was beyond him.

This wasn't the first missing husband case he'd worked on since becoming a private investigator. It was his bread and butter, in fact. Usually, when a wife wanted their husband tracked down, he found them exactly where the wife suspected them to be. At the home of another woman.

But this case was different. After speaking to Mrs. Carroll, who seemed to know beyond a shadow of a doubt that her husband would never be unfaithful, Kyle went around town asking others about the character of Daniel Carroll. He'd worked for a lot of women in the past who thought their husbands would never cheat on them either. Most of the time they were wrong. It was disheartening. Did anyone take marriage seriously anymore? He would, if he ever found the right woman.

Everyone he spoke to, said the same thing about Daniel Carroll. He loved his wife more than anything, and there was no way he'd do anything like that.

While it was possible to fool the whole world into thinking you're someone you're not, he'd never known a man to have a reputation like Daniel Carroll.

"A good Christian man," "A Godly man." Everyone had similar things to say about him. It was nice to hear that good people still existed. The fact that this man hadn't been seen or heard from by his wife took this case in a different direction. One that explained the feeling of dread that puddled in the bottom of his stomach.

High stepping his way through the thick brush made the muscles in his thighs burn and ache. It took him several minutes to finally make it to the clearing. The stone structure he'd seen through the trees was an old chimney. At the bottom was a stone mantel and fireplace.

He'd read about places like this before. There used to be a house here a long time ago. From what he could tell, they had built the house in a bowl. He knew these woods were part of a historical park, but there didn't seem to be any path or trail leading to this historic site. Surely the property owners knew this was here.

It took a few minutes of careful steps in the right places to make it down the little incline. Once he was at the bottom, the stone chimney stood much higher. It was a lot bigger than it looked.

He approached it and stood directly in front of it. This was either the home of a very large family or a meeting house of some kind. He'd seen other stone chimneys in the past and they weren't half the size of this one.

Could this be the reason Daniel Carroll was in the woods so much? It was perfectly secluded and peaceful. Only the sounds of nature tickled the ear. Yes, this would be the perfect place to come when one wanted to shut out the world. He could see himself coming to a place like this often to think and talk to God.  Still, an eerie feeling crept up the back of his neck, like someone was watching him.

As he turned to go back to his search, something moved in his peripheral vision. He took a peek in that direction. Who knows what kind of animal he could meet out here? He froze for about ten seconds. Nothing else moved. He was just about to investigate when his phone vibrated in his pocket.

He looked down as he tried to dig it out. It was probably Mrs. Carroll again, asking if he'd found her husband yet. It would be the third time she'd called today. Before he could get the phone out to answer it, a flash lit up the forest. It came from the same direction as the movement. He was right. Someone had been watching him.

"Stupid flash," Someone muttered. The muscle in his jaw twitched as he stood frozen. The phone call would have to wait. He let it fall back down into his pocket, waiting for an opportunity to get his hands on whoever this was.

The thicket they were hiding behind was about twenty feet away. That gave them a pretty good head start. Maybe he could get the drop on them. Come at them when they least expect it. The flash and the muffled speech told him they were nervous. That gave him the advantage he needed.

He peeked out of the corner of his eye in the flash's direction. No movement. This was it. He turned and took long strides, taking an extra precaution to make sure his steps were silent. Only a few more feet. He had them. They wouldn't be able to outrun him now.

"Hold it, right there!" He stopped in his tracks, slowly raising his hands. A woman popped out from behind a tree. Her long auburn hair spilled over the shoulders of her black jacket. She was in a navy blue pencil skirt and flats. What really had his attention was the barrel he was staring down. She was a fair distance from where he'd seen the movement. How did she get from behind the thicket to behind that tree? How did she do it without him noticing? Yes, the woods were thick, but not that thick.

"Take it easy," He kept his hands up, watching for any physical cues of what her next move would be.

"You're trespassing," She stated.

"Technically, yes, but I'm looking for someone. I was told he comes out here a lot,"

"Who are you looking for?"

"Daniel Carroll. You know him?" She nodded behind the handgun that was still pointed at him.

"He's my uncle," She responded.

"Ok. Your aunt Bertha hired me to find him." She spoke before he could continue.

"That's a lie. I saw him yesterday morning,"

"She hired me last night,"

"That makes zero sense," She fired back.

"Well, it would make more sense if you'd let me explain." He instantly regretted those words. He needed to remember she had a handgun pointed at him. No matter how distracting her flowing hair was. He wasn't sure if she was the type of woman who had what it took to pull the trigger if necessary, and he didn't want to find out.

"Save it. You can explain it to the cops." She whipped the barrel to the left, indicating the direction she wanted him to go. Great. That was the one thing he wanted to avoid. Speaking to the cops meant he would have to see his brother. His mind raced, trying to come up with a way of getting out of the situation. He wasn't ready to face Michael again.

A loud gasp and shriek caused him to freeze once again.

"Uncle Dan!" He turned. The woman was kneeling about eight feet from where she stood a moment earlier. He went to her side. On the ground, behind another thicket was a middle-aged man wearing a blue Civil War uniform. He was lying on his side, and his face was white. He'd been gone for several hours. Looks like Daniel Carroll was out here after all.

# CHAPTER 2

She glanced up in time to witness his eyes widen like dinner plates at the sight of her uncle's corpse. Her heart plummeted, but she kept her cool. She was alone in a forest with a potential murderer.

"Did you do this?" The words escaped her lips before she could think it through.

"No! I told you. Bertha Carroll hired me to find him." He pointed at Uncle Dan. She stood to her feet, pointing her pistol at him again. Her mind became a jumbled mess. She had to get the cops out here. They would go to the Arbutus House and see her car there, but would they search for her? Would she make it out of here alive?

This guy acted just as shocked as she did to see Uncle Dan lying there. As if he'd just seen the body for the first time. That was a good sign he was telling the truth, wasn't it? Her heart beat against her ribs. The force made her breath heavier. A small part of her felt that this man was being honest. That he could be trusted. His dark blue-green eyes had kindness to them.

*A big risk to take on a feeling.*

His lips parted, as if to say something more, but a whizzing sound in the air near her head cut him off. Without thinking, she ducked down and spun her neck around, hoping to determine where it came from.

The man across from her gun barrel fell. He gripped her wrist and tugged her behind a tree. She yelped in pain, a piercing sound. His strong hold on her arm kept her from running when she tried to break free.

"I wouldn't do that if I were you," he said, peeking slightly around the tree. Another round smashed into the tree. Her car wasn't far. She could make it if she kept her head down.

"Let go of me," She growled. He held his grip, looking off in another direction.

"Get ready to run on the count of three," His voice had taken on a commanding tone. She decided not to argue. She peered over his shoulder in the direction he was looking. He'd parked a black SUV on the side of the road about thirty yards away from where they were hiding. She had no idea how she missed that.

"Three!" He blurted out, pulling on her wrist again. Her first instinct was to cover her head with her arm. She ducked down as low as she could while continuing to follow this stranger. She had no choice but to follow him. All the horror stories of abduction came to mind. Would this lead to her ending up just like Uncle Dan? Two more shots echoed through the forest. He led her around to the other side of the vehicle and shoved her inside just as another shot hit the side.

It took him only a few seconds to get into the driver's seat. Meg brushed the hair from her face just as the SUV lurched forward, getting them away from the shooter. Her heart was still pounding. The stillness of the car only magnified just how hard it was beating.

"What in the world is going on?" Her voice broke as she spoke.

"I honestly don't know," He scratched the back of his neck as if trying to figure it out. A lump formed in her throat as the image of Uncle Dan laying on the forest floor flashed in her mind. He was gone. She'd never see him again. Part of her wanted to break down right there, but she had to remember that she wasn't out of harm's way yet. She still didn't know this guy's name.

"Who are you?" She could see his shoulders moving up and down as he wheezed. Was he as scared as she was or just out of breath? She knew to watch body language in order to tell what someone was thinking. Now she was going to put what her mom had taught her to the test. His body slightly stiffened.

"Kyle," he said slowly.

"Kyle what? I asked you who you are. You wanted the opportunity to explain. Now you've got it. Spill!"

"My name is Kyle Redman. I'm a private investigator. I was hired by Bertha Carroll to find her husband, Daniel. This job did not end the way I thought it would," His tone changed in the middle of his speaking as if he'd gone from talking to her, to talking to himself.

"Any relation to Michael Redman?" She asked.

"He's my brother," She let his response roll around in her mind. She'd known Michael and Jessica Redman for a few years. Jessica was an only child, but she had no idea Michael had a brother. She wanted to trust him based on that alone, but knew that wasn't wise. Yes, siblings were often a lot alike, but there were some cases where siblings were total opposites. Which was probably why Michael never mentioned his brother.

Even though she didn't know this man. Something about him made her feel safe. Like she could trust him. Now she had lost it. This guy was a complete stranger and possibly her uncle's killer. He could've even made up the story about being Michael's brother. She'd seen a few episodes on the Crime show channel about murderers claiming to be family members in order to learn where to find their intended victims.

The car jolted forward as they came to a stop. They were in front of the Oakwood Springs PD. She hadn't even realized they'd gone that far. Kyle stared at the front door, drew in a deep breath, then blew it out. Was he nervous about seeing Michael? He turned, keeping his gaze on the seat belt lock as he unbuckled. She couldn't tell for sure from all the movement, but it looked like his lip was slightly quivering. Whatever was going through his mind seemed to make him forget that she was there.

Everything inside the Oakwood Springs PD seemed to be running the same as usual. It made her insides ache. The world would go on without Uncle Dan as if he was never here. A sob threatened to erupt from her throat. She quickly swallowed it as she opened the door to Clayton Denny's office.

"Megan, are you alright?" Clay was circling his desk as she let the door swing open. Relief washed over her at the sight of a familiar face. Clay grabbed her shoulders and pulled her into a hug, just like her dad would. Genuine worry was in his eyes. She was sure she'd get the same reaction once her dad got here.

"I'm fine, Uncle Clay," She responded. Fine on the outside, maybe, but inside, she was about to lose it.

"Uncle Dan has been murdered," She blurted out, bursting into tears.

*****

Kyle's eyebrows shot up as he watched the officer embrace her. She proceeded to tell him what had happened in the last hour; their meeting, the shooter and the movement she spotted from the window of a historic house. Kyle had steered clear of that place, meaning the only person she could've seen was the killer.

Judging by the way the officer glared over her shoulder, things weren't looking good for him. Whoever this woman was, she was well-connected and could bring him trouble. He had to leave town as soon as possible. He'd tell Bertha Carroll that he found her husband, get his money, and hit the road. Hopefully, he'd be miles away before Michael got word that he was in town in the first place.

He was just about to say something when the barrel-chested officer moved Megan aside and approached him with a look that sent a chill down Kyle's spine. Even though he looked to be twice Kyle's age. Clay wasn't someone he wanted to mess with. He was more than a foot taller than Kyle, and his shoulders were twice as wide. It was a wonder how he fit through the door.

"You mind telling me who you are?" His tone was gruff. Great. He would have to announce his presence to the entire town before this was over. It was only a matter of time before Michael found out he was here.

"His name is Kyle Redman. He's Michael Redman's brother," Meg volunteered. She looked at him, almost as if seeking approval for offering the information to him. The officer looked over his shoulder at her.

"Your parents are on their way. You can wait for them in my office," he said. There was an underlying message in his tone. It was a safe guess to say he was telling her to back up and let him handle things. She didn't protest. Kyle would've taken it as being treated like a child. She didn't seem like the type to go for that, but she had. Maybe she wasn't the strong woman she portrayed.

"Come with me, Mr. Redman. I have some questions for you," Clay said as he stomped by. Just as he turned to follow him, there was movement out of the corner of his eye.

"Kyle?!" Michael stood in the doorway just to his right. He seemed happy to see him. A lot happier than Kyle expected him to be. Michael marched toward him and pulled him into a tight hug.

"Oh my gosh! I can't believe you're here! How long are you in town for?" Before Kyle could answer, Clay approached them, placing a hand on his shoulder.

"He's a suspect in a murder investigation," he said to Michael.

The statement seemed to surprise him at first, but the wide-eyed expression quickly turned into a condescending smile. Clay's face reddened. His frown deepened.

*Wrong move Bro,*

"What makes him a suspect? What evidence have you found?" Michael asked, crossing his arms. Michael hadn't lost his know-it-all behavior. Clay gritted his teeth, then took a step back from him.

"I was going to ask him some questions while a team investigated the crime scene," Clay growled. It was easy to see that he didn't like being under Michael. That was one area where he could relate.

"I'll ask the questions," Michael stated, motioning him into his office. He'd grown up dealing with Michael's I-know-more-than-you side. This was one time he was thankful for it.

Before entering Michael's office, he glanced over his shoulder just in time to see Megan follow Clay outside. Michael closed the door.

"You're lucky I overheard what was going on" His brother gave him a pointed side glance.

"What's his deal? I bring that woman in here after saving her life and I'm on trial all of a sudden," Kyle burst out. Getting her to safety gave him that heroic feeling their dad always talked about. He didn't get to feel it as often as Michael did, but it came from time to time. Now, the victorious feeling was short-lived.

"Calm down. He's just very protective of her,".

"Who is she anyway?" Kyle asked, just realizing that he hadn't caught her name.

"Megan Holmes. Goes by Meg. She's a reporter for the newspaper. Her parents own A tourist attraction just outside of town. A Civil War house where one of the battles took place. They do reenactments and stuff."

"That explains the uniform,"

"Uniform?" Michael asked.

"Yeah, he was wearing a Union Officer uniform," Michael's eyes widened, then turned to disbelief.

"Daniel Carroll used to play a union officer. But he hasn't in over a year. He had an accident with a horse, so he had to stop."

"Well, that's what he was wearing."

Kyle's cases went a lot smoother when he had the help of the local police department. They had access to criminal records and tech he didn't. This was one time he wished he could solve the case all on his own. Whatever happened here, the credit would likely go to Michael.

When they were kids, their mom told them about when Jesus spoke about the root of bitterness. It can borrow deep in the heart and be nearly impossible to get out, especially without the help of Christ. For Kyle, it was more of a thorny vine that wrapped around his insides, stabbing him and cutting him deeply with every move he made.

The thought made his insides tense. He would have to be prepared for the pain that vine would bring him as long as he was in Oakwood Springs.

# CHAPTER 3

Megan climbed into Clay's car, unsure of what just happened. She'd known Clay her entire life, why did he act so weird to Kyle? She'd never seen him charge like that at anyone before, or decide on the spot that someone was guilty. Seeing him that way worried her. Scared her even. Did he know something about him that she didn't? She stole a quick glance at him while he had his phone to his ear.

Apparently, a K-9 unit and the coroner would meet them at the Arbutus House. After he ended his call, he placed his phone in the cupholder between them.

"Do you know Kyle Redman?" She asked. The deep frown returned to his face.

"Why?" His question came out in a low hum that resembled a growl.

"Because you charged at him like a bull, and I can't help but think that you would've locked him up on the spot if you could." Clay was a just man. She'd seen him work with so many people, helping them get their lives on track. What was it about this man that sent her uncle into a rage at the mere sight of him?

We deal with all kinds of people. I just can't stand it when a shady drifter comes to town and brings a big mess with them. We've got good, God-fearing people here. I won't stand by and let one of them get hurt. Especially not my niece."

"He's Michael Redman's brother. I doubt he'd be that shady. Plus, we don't know if he brought the shooter here. This has something to do with Uncle Dan." Her voice cracked as she spoke the last few words. It still hadn't sunk in that he was gone. It probably never would.

"So you believe his story about Bertha bringing him here?"

"I think it's worth checking out. Innocent until proven guilty. Right?" His jaw twitched. She could tell he was muddling over her words.

"Yes. But not you. I'll go talk to her as soon as we're done at the crime scene,"

Normally, Meg would be in the middle of all the action. Experiencing it up close made it easier to write sensational stories with lots of detail. She held up her hands.

"Alright, fine. It's your investigation." She tried to sound as lighthearted as possible, hoping it would lift Clay out of his funk. Disappointment settled over her when it didn't work.

"Listen, when we get there, I'm going to take a few officers to make sure the area is secure. You stay in the car until I say it's clear. You got that?"

She gave him a dip of her head in response. His gruff expression softened.

Clay made the turn down the little side road that was only a mile from the Arbutus House. A wave of nausea hit her as the entrance of the parking lot came into view. What if they were still out here? Watching. Waiting for their next target. She barely made it out alive earlier. She might not be so lucky this time.

She took a deep breath, forcing her stomach to relax. The house came into view. Her car was parked right where she left it. She'd half expected it to have gotten stolen. The fact that it wasn't spoke volumes. This wasn't someone out to steal from the historic site. They pursued them with the intent of killing them. That was their purpose for being out here. That meant only one thing. This was personal. She had to reconsider Clay's words about Kyle bringing this killer to town with him. Surely they weren't after her.

Clay pulled up next to her car and shut the engine off. At that angle, she could see a spider web-shaped shatter on her windshield. Next to it was a yellow sticky note plastered to the window by the moist air. She took a few steps closer to her car. She wanted to be able to get away if someone leaped out of it or from behind it at her. Her blood ran icy as she read the words written on the sticky note.

I'M COMING FOR YOU

They were after her. This really had nothing to do with Kyle. Unless he'd been the one to put it there. She'd heard of cases where the killer would pretend to be a friend of their next victim. Using their emotions against them like a cat with a toy.

She looked over her shoulder to Clay. He climbed out a quickly joined her. He blew out an angry breath, then wiped his hand across his mouth.

"I'm going to call this in real quick. One fingerprint is all we need," He was still in the mindset that Kyle was the one behind this. She climbed back into the car with him as he reported the vandalism and threatening note.

"They should be out here in a few minutes. Now, show me where you found this guy snooping."

Seeing her car tampered with made her wonder if he was still hiding out here, waiting to end her life. She had her weapon on her, but wanted more protection before traipsing through the wood a second time today, especially now that she knew she'd been the target the whole time.

"Okay. I want to get something out of the trunk of my car first. Keep watch for me?" Clay smiled and nodded.

He looked after her all her life. He was one of the few people she trusted to watch her back while she got her bulletproof vest out of the trunk of her car. Not only would it protect her from standard-size bullets. It would also help her keep her nerves in check while trying to retrace her steps.

It didn't take them long to get back to the spot where Kyle had been looking at the remaining rubble of the historic cabin in the woods. Replaying the events of the day kind of made her wish he was here. But that was a natural reaction to meeting a good-looking guy. There wasn't anything more to it than that.

Clay went to where she'd told him Kyle was standing when she topped the little ridge. He scanned the surrounding ground, took a few steps, then scanned some more.

"What are you looking for?"

"Nothing in particular. Anything that isn't supposed to be there." He looked for a few more seconds. Silence settled between them. She was nearly holding her breath, as if any noise would prevent Clay from finding anything suspicious.

"Like this, for example," He said, crouching down beside a bush that was less than two yards from where Kyle had been standing. Meg quickly joined him. She froze. Unable to breathe.

The butt of a rifle stuck out from under the thicket. It looked like someone dropped it, then kicked it under it.

*****

He was hoping to be in and out of Oakwood Springs without bumping into Michael. But it seemed like God had other plans. Michael seemed to put the past behind him. No comments about how he had disappointed their parents, or about how he didn't think Kyle was really trying to accomplish anything serious in his life.

Did he know how badly his words hurt? Kyle had always been a bit of a class clown, but the jokester would only spring to life in times of great stress. It was what he hated most about himself. Keeping that part of him at bay meant that there wasn't much laughter in his life. He also felt that he'd grown up a bit too. That was the side he wanted Michael to see, but the stress of getting rejected or called a disappointment by his only brother was more than he could handle sometimes.

He had no idea that he'd receive the greeting from Michael that he had. He was almost certain that it was the first time Michael had ever hugged him, like really hugged him.

Kyle drove past the turnoff that led to the Civil War house as he followed the GPS directions. Michael gave him his address and told him to go to his house and that he'd meet him there. He would try to smooth things over with Meg's uncle so he wouldn't be charged with a murder he had nothing to do with.

"You can stay with Jess and me until we can officially clear you of everything,"

Michael had said before he left.

"And if you can't?"

"Then I know a good attorney," Michael's optimism was comforting, but it didn't seem to be enough. He still felt off. His mind went to Bertha Carroll. Technically She'd hired him to find her husband, and things were different, he could see them being friends.

"You've arrived at your destination," The GPS said. The robotic voice made him jump.

To his left, a cute yellow house with red shutters came into view. He instantly recognized Michael's pickup truck. Kyle parked his car next to it and took a deep breath before getting out. He wasn't sure what to expect or how much Michael had told his wife Jess about Kyle's situation. Would she think him innocent or guilty?

He walked up to the bright red door and knocked. After a few seconds, the door opened to reveal a smiling Jess. Her petite frame was clothed in jeans and a white blouse that made her seem even tinier. Black hair, tamed into two side braids, framed her face while her gentle brown eyes smiled at him only for a second before she gave him a brotherly side hug.

"Come in, come in, I just got off the phone with Michael, he told me what happened. How are you holding up?"

"I'm doing okay, thanks. Just taking things one step at a time. I'll be happy when this case is solved." Kyle was taken aback by her warmth and genuine concern.

Jess led him to the kitchen where the warm earthy aroma of Folger's Black Silk.

"Coffee?"

Kyle nodded, and Jess poured him a cup. They sat down at the table, and Jess brought over a plate of cookies.

"Why don't you tell me what happened?" Jess suggested as she picked up a cookie.

"I thought you said Michael told you what happened?"

"He did, but I want to hear it from you," Jess took another bite of the gooey cookie.

Kyle took a sip of the hot coffee, grateful for the warmth. He took a deep breath before starting his story. Jess already knew everything, from the moment Bertha Carroll hired him to find her husband, to the discovery of the body and the subsequent events that led him to Oakwood Springs. He even told her about his run-in with Meg and how he was now a suspect in her uncle's murder.

Jess listened intently, her expression never wavering. When he finished, she reached across the table and took his hand. "I'm sorry you've been through all of this, Kyle. It sounds like a nightmare."

Kyle nodded.

"It has been, but I'm just trying to take things one step at a time. I want to find the person who killed Daniel Carroll and clear my name in the process."

Jess squeezed his hand.

"I believe you can do it. And you have Michael and me on your side to help in any way we can." Kyle felt a lump form in his throat at her kindness. He didn't know Jess all that well, but he could see that she was a genuine person who cared about others.

"Thank you, Jess. That means a lot to me."

She smiled at him.

"Of course, Kyle. We're family, and that's what family does for each other."

Kyle felt a sense of warmth spread through his chest. Maybe things would work out after all. He took another sip of coffee and smiled back at Jess.

As he set his coffee cup down, a knock at the door interrupted their conversation. Jess got up to answer it, and Kyle heard a familiar voice greet her, followed by the smacking sound of a kiss.

Michael entered the kitchen, looking a bit worn out. Kyle stood up to meet him, feeling a bit nervous despite their earlier embrace.

"I spoke with the DA. There is only circumstantial evidence against Kyle right now, and she told me it wouldn't be enough to take to court against him. So we are in the clear for now."

"Well, I guess that's somewhat good news." Jess chimed in.

Michael nodded in agreement, then turned his attention back to Kyle. "I need you to tell me what happened out there again. The smallest detail might help us find the real killer,"

Kyle took a deep breath and recounted his story again, focusing on the details that he hadn't shared before, like how Daniel's body was positioned in the high grass.

"There was also a weird smell. I've smelled it before but I can't remember where, "Michael listened intently, nodding at certain points and asking clarifying questions.

When Kyle finished, Michael stood up and walked over to the window, staring out at the yard. "This is a tough one," he said finally. "There's not much to go on. But we'll figure it out. We have to."

# CHAPTER 4

Meg swallowed hard as she flipped on her left blinker. The sun was fading in the sky, and she wanted more than anything to forget this day ever happened. Her body felt heavy with exhaustion, but she couldn't go home until she'd told Kyle what they had found. No evidence suggested he was responsible for this crime - yet something inside of her whispered that it wasn't him. If not him, then who? Somebody had intentionally framed him - but who, and why?

Clay would lead this investigation because the prime suspect was the sheriff's brother, but deep down she knew Clay wanted the position of mayor with the same desperation as a drowning man wants air. He'd do anything at this point to ensure the people of Oakwood Springs that he would do a better job than Michael, even if it meant throwing an innocent man under the bus. She wanted justice for Uncle Dan, but not at the expense of the innocent, and refused to let that happen. She navigated her car into the sheriff's driveway. The sound of gravel crunching beneath her tires seemed deafening in the quiet neighborhood street; every little sound magnified until it was like a gunshot echoing through her head.

Taking a deep breath, she got out of the car and walked up to the front door. She hesitated for a moment before knocking. Her heart fluttered as she pictured Kyle sitting on the couch. His golden blonde hair glistened under the light.

*Get a hold of yourself.*

She was acting like a teenager with a crush. Meg straightened her shoulders and knocked on the door. After a few seconds, it opened and Kyle stood before her, looking surprised to see her.

"Meg, what are you doing here?" Kyle asked, confusion etched on his face.

"I needed to talk to you," Meg replied, her voice barely above a whisper.
Kyle gestured for her to come in, and they walked into the living room. Meg took a seat on the couch, and Kyle sat across from her in a matching armchair.

"Meg, It's great to see you!" Jess and Michael entered the living room from the kitchen.

"Is everything okay?" Michael asked.

"Actually, no," she responded.

"Clay took me back to the Arbutus House to get my car. He wanted me to show him where I found you in the woods. He looked around out there and found a rifle right where you were standing. Clay is sure it's the murder weapon and is having it checked for fingerprints. He feels that should be enough to charge you with Uncle Dan's murder." She explained.

Kyle's eyes widened.

"What? That's ridiculous," he exclaimed.

"I know," Meg said, her voice shaking slightly. "That's why I came here. I wanted to make sure you heard it from me. I don't believe you did it, Kyle."

Kyle leaned forward in his chair, his expression intense.

Kyle ran a hand through his hair, looking frustrated. "This is insane. I need to clear my name."

Jess sat down on the couch next to Meg, placing a comforting hand on her shoulder. "We'll help you, Kyle. We're all in this together."

Michael nodded in agreement. "We'll start by looking into anyone who might have wanted Daniel Carroll dead."

That was easier said than done. Everyone who knew Daniel Carroll thought he was the sweetest person. Everyone loved him and respected him.

"Let's not forget the part where the culprit was trying to kill Meg as well," Kyle added.

"Are we certain that she was the target? He might have been after both of you,"

"I'm the target," Meg muttered, the words almost took her breath away from fear.

"How do you know?" Jess asked her.

"Because there's something else," All eyes turned to her.

"There was a note on my windshield when I went back to get my car. ," The new clue piqued Kyles' interest even more.

"What did it say?"

"I'm coming for you. It was written in all caps."

"So that tells us without a doubt that you were the target," Jess pushed an ebony strand behind her ear.

Meg looked at Jess to agree, but didn't form the words. Something was off about

Jess. There was an air about her that said she wasn't well. As she watched her for a moment, she noticed Jess was taking short, rapid breaths. Neither one of the men seemed to notice she was sick.

"Jess, are you feeling okay?" Meg interrupted Michael. He turned his attention to his wife. Jess offered a big smile.

"Totally." Meg didn't believe her, but Jess raised her eyebrows slightly. Her eyes pleaded for Meg to drop the subject.

"It's getting close to dinnertime. How about I order a pizza?" Jess got up and started for the kitchen.

"Meg, why don't you come and tell me what your favorite toppings are?" She stood and followed Jess. She didn't know Jess that well, but one woman didn't have to know another to understand the woman code. It was as if God gave women the ability to speak this secret language to one another. It especially came in handy when someone needed help that they can't get from their husband or dad.

Jess's phone was on the corner of the countertop, next to the sliding door where it was plugged into a charger. The dim orange light that covered the backyard told Meg that it would be dark soon. Maybe she should ask someone to make sure she got home okay.

*No, don't be a baby. You can take care of yourself.*

Jess picked up her phone and took a step back, so they were out of the men's sight. She leaned in and spoke in a whisper.

"Please don't say anything. But yes, I'm not feeling well at all right now."

Meg felt her eyes get wider.

"Why not? Don't you think you should tell your husband?"

"I will. But I'm pregnant and I want to tell him in a special way," The tired, sick look on Jess's face seemed to transform into that pregnancy glow she'd always heard about. Her chest filled with a gasp. It was something she always marveled at. How the news of a pregnancy sparks so much excitement, even in the people you aren't close to.

Jess brought her index finger to her lips. Meg winked at her.

"Your secret's safe with me,"

Meg went back into the living room as Jess tapped the screen of her phone.

Michael wore a look of concern. Did he hear what Jess said? There was no doubt that he sensed something was wrong with her, too.

"What's up?"

"It looks like pepperoni and sausage,"

"Sounds great to me," Kyle chimed in. Meg couldn't help but notice the warm, safe feeling settling over her. That sense of family. Of belonging. She had no reason to feel that way, as they weren't family at all.

She stole a glance at Kyle, who she immediately noticed was watching her as well. What would it be like to be part of his life permanently?

*****

Kyle had a difficult time sorting through his emotions. He was trying to get through the awkward feeling between him and his brother while fighting his attraction to Meg.

"I can only imagine what Dad would say if he were here." He'd been the family's disappointment for most of his life. Why should he expect things to change? Michael pulled his attention from the kitchen, where Jess was still on the phone with Pizza Hut.

"What do you mean?"

"I failed the police academy, I ran off and became a PI, and now I'm the prime suspect in a murder investigation. Guess there are things you can't change about yourself, no matter how badly you want to."

Kyle felt a feminine hand on top of his. He looked up to meet Meg's gaze.

"Kyle, you're not a disappointment. You're a good guy. And we'll prove your innocence in this case."

Kyle smiled weakly at her. He appreciated her words, but he couldn't shake the feeling of failure that seemed to follow him everywhere.

"I know I've been a bit of a prodigal son, but at least his dad welcomed him back with open arms,"

"And what makes you think our dad won't do the same thing?" Michael asked. Jess came back into the living room, phone in hand. "Pizza will be here in 20 minutes," she announced, sitting down next to Michael.

Those 20 minutes seemed to fly by. Michael met the pizza delivery guy and brought in the flat box. The aroma made his stomach rumble. Everyone ate in silence. But it was evident on each face that the wheels were turning.

Meg stood after eating only one slice.

"I hate to eat and run, but I need to get home."

Kyle looked up at Meg, a sense of disappointment washing over him. He had been hoping to spend more time with her, to figure out what he was feeling and how to deal with it. But he knew that Meg had to leave, and he wasn't going to hold her back.

"Let me drive you home. You out alone isn't a good idea right now," Kyle said, standing up from the couch.

"I'll be fine from here to the car and from my car to my house."

"Then at least let me walk you to your car," He responded. She smiled.

"Thanks," She said goodbye to Michael and Jess, winking at his sister-in-law. Was there something up their sleeves or was that just a woman thing? He'd probably never know.

# CHAPTER 5

Meg couldn't wait to get into bed and put this day behind her. It had been a nightmare from start to finish. She closed her parents' front door behind her and went into the kitchen to see if there was anything chocolate to eat. She'd earned it after everything she'd been through.

"Megan? Is that you?" she heard her mother's voice from the kitchen. She should've known her mom would still be up. She spent a lot of time sanitizing the house and medical equipment for her dad. It had basically become her life after her father's accident. It quickly got tough for her to care for him by herself, which was why Meg moved back home. She could help her dad get down to the Arbutus house for events and to work behind the host desk.

"Yeah, Mom, it's me," She responded. The second she entered the kitchen, she was greeted by her mom's tightest hug and sobs.

"I heard what happened. Are you alright? I would've come down there, but there wasn't anyone to sit with your dad."

"I'm fine, Mom really." She gave her a comforting rub on the back.

"Your dad is beside himself with all this. Losing Uncle Dan and nearly losing you."

"Is he still up? I'd like to see him before I go to bed," Meg started up the stairs. The chocolate treat would have to wait. Her Dad hadn't been the same since the day the doctors told him he'd never walk again. She knocked on his door.

"Dad? You still up."

"Come in," her dad's voice was weak. Meg opened the door and saw him lying in his hospital bed, watching TV. His eyes lit up when he saw her.

"Meg, thank God you're okay," he said, his voice breaking.

"I'm fine, Dad. I just wanted to check on you before I went to bed." Her dad patted the bed next to him.

"Come sit with me." Meg sat down next to her dad and he put his arm around her. They sat there in silence for a while, just enjoying each other's company.

"I don't know what I'd do if I lost you," he said, his voice barely above a whisper.

"Dad, I'm sorry for worrying you," she said, sitting down next to him.

"It's not your fault, Meg. I just wish I could've done something to protect you and Dan," her dad replied, placing a hand on hers.

Meg felt a pang of guilt in her chest. She knew her dad blamed himself for the accident that had left him paralyzed and unable to protect his family.

"You did everything you could, Dad. And I'm okay, thanks to Kyle and Michael," she reassured him.

Her dad sighed, "I know, but it doesn't make it any easier. There have been a lot of people over the years who turned against you since you started working for the newspaper. It scares me. Like Victor Bradford from last year."

Maryann Baker wasn't the first person to tell her she'd be sorry for something she wrote. Victor used to own a huge apartment complex in town, but he was under investigation for a murder that took place in one of his apartments. Most of his tenants moved out after her article was published in the paper. He lost the complex and his own home not long after that.

"Victor was just mad about losing his house. He doesn't seem like the murderer type."

"They never do," He responded. He was right, and she knew that. That was one aspect of this case that no one had thought of before. She had made enemies through the paper, Victor was only the youngest. But was he a killer?

Meg sat with her dad for a while, talking about the upcoming events at the Arbutus house. Eventually, he fell asleep and Meg quietly left the room, heading back to her bedroom.

As she lay in bed, Meg couldn't get Kyle out of her head. She didn't know what it was about him, but something drew her to him. She tried to push the thoughts away, knowing it was a bad idea to get involved with a suspect in a murder investigation.

But as she closed her eyes, she couldn't help but imagine what it would be like to be in Kyle's arms. She was nearly asleep when a scream echoed through the house. Her mother's scream. She threw back the blanket and scrambled to her feet. Not her mom.

*Please, God.*

Meg grabbed her handgun from her bed and ran down the stairs as quickly as she could. When she entered the kitchen. Her mom was on the floor in a sitting position. Both hands were pressed tightly to her chest.

"Mom, are you okay? Are you hurt?"

She shook her head no to both questions. Several thuds shook the room. Her dad was tapping on the floor with his stick. Of course, he'd be concerned as well but he would have to wait.

"What happened?"

"Someone came up behind me and grabbed me. They were trying to get me out the door, but I managed to scream. They dropped me and ran off," The explanation came out in hiccups and sobs. Meg felt as if someone had lit her insides on fire. First, her uncle, now her mom? She couldn't figure out what this person was after. Why did he want to hurt two of the sweetest people in town?

Meg put her mom's arm over her shoulders and helped the sixty-two-year-old get to her feet.

"Come on. I'll take you to your room. You can tell Dad what happened while I call the police," This only made things more complicated. They hadn't figured out who would want Dan dead, now they are after her mom. She wasn't sure how much more of this she could take.

*****

Kyle did his best to try to make the couch comfortable, but it was futile. The hard cushions felt like he was laying in stone. He pulled the blanket a little higher, then dropped it back on his lap when he felt someone shoving his arm.

"Kyle, wake up!" It was Michael, looking agitated. "Something's happened at Meg's house."

Kyle sat up, instantly alert. "What happened?"

"I don't know all the details, but Meg's mom was attacked. A few officers are on their way over there now."

Kyle jumped up from the couch, pulling his shirt back on. "Let's go."

The two of them rushed out of Michael's apartment and headed for Meg's house. As they walked, Kyle's mind raced. Who would want to hurt Meg's mom? Was it related to Dan's murder? Or was it something else entirely?

When they arrived at the house, Meg was standing outside, talking to a police officer. She looked tense and worried. Kyle felt a pang of sympathy for her.

"Meg," he said, rushing over to her. "Are you okay?"

She nodded, but her eyes were wide with fear. "My mom's in shock, but physically she's okay. The police are inside talking to her and my dad."

"What happened?" Michael asked.

"She said somebody tried to grab her and drag her out of the house," Meg said, her voice shaking. "But she screamed, and they dropped her and ran off. I don't know who it was or why they did it."

Kyle's fists clenched in rage. The urge to find the perpetrator and exact revenge was almost overpowering, but he forced himself to take a deep breath and push his emotions aside. He had to think rationally if he wanted to help Meg and her mom.

"Did you see anything?" he asked Meg.

She shook her head. "I was upstairs in my room."

He watched as she placed her shaking hand over her mouth and shut her eyes tight, a single tear slipping down her cheek. He felt his chest tighten with grief at the sight of her pain.

"Meg, we are going to get this guy. I promise you."

She looked up at him, her eyes searching his face. "Thank you, Kyle. I know that solving this case is just as critical for you as it is for me."

Kyle felt a sense of warmth in his chest at her words. He wrapped an arm around her shoulders, pulling her close. "We're not going anywhere. We'll do whatever it takes to keep you and your family safe."

Meg leaned into him, her body trembling with emotion. Kyle felt a surge of protectiveness wash over him. He would do whatever it took to keep her safe, even if it meant putting himself in danger.

As they stood there, wrapped in each other's arms, Kyle couldn't help but feel strange. He'd known this woman less than twenty-four hours, but he was undeniably attracted to her. He would have to bury it. Getting involved with a suspect in a murder investigation was the worst thing he could do right now.

But as he looked down at Meg's tear-streaked face, some invisible force drew him near. He leaned down and kissed her, his lips soft and gentle against hers.

Meg responded eagerly, her arms wrapping around his neck as she deepened the kiss. Michael came down the stairs from the interview with her parents.

He cleared his throat, interrupting them. Kyle broke the kiss and turned to face his brother, feeling a little embarrassed.

"Sorry about that," he said, rubbing the back of his neck.

Michael grinned at him, but said nothing.

Kyle turned back to Meg, his eyes locking onto hers. "I shouldn't have done that. I'm sorry."

"I'm sorry too. I should go check on my parents," Meg said, hurrying past them.

The moment Meg was out of sight, Michael turned to him. He expected him to comment on the kiss, but he didn't.

"I spoke to the parents, and they said Meg gets a lot of threats after writing certain stories for the paper."

"You think this might be someone making good on their threats?" Kyle asked.

"Could be. It's a start, anyway. They said Victor Bradford needs to be checked out first, but I noticed something."

"What?"

"Meg and her mom both have long red hair, and they were both wearing a forest green shirt this evening,"

"You think this is a mistake in identity??" That wasn't the direction he was thinking, but it seemed like Michael was on the right path. All the clues were adding up.

Hopefully, an arrest could be made soon.

92

# CHAPTER 6

If only life had a pause button. That way, work could be put on hold and she could spend every minute finding Uncle Dan's killer. It was Thursday, which meant it was her turn in the upstairs office, taking phone calls and bookkeeping. Her article for the Oakwood Post was due in a few days, so she had to work on that at the same time. She could only pray that Kyle and Michael would find the killer.

Her fingers were sore. She looked down at her hands. They were in tight fists again, making her knuckles turn white. She shook her hands, forcing the blood to return to them. She wanted so badly to call and see if they'd found anything. Not knowing what was going on was driving her crazy.

Meg closed her eyes and drew in a deep breath. It had been two days since Kyle promised he would catch the guy. Two days since the killer nearly took her mother's life. She had to trust Kyle. Trust him to keep his word and find this person. It would be the first time in her life that she trusted someone with something so important.

She couldn't get over the special way she felt when around him. He was smart and funny and utterly gorgeous and, if she was really honest with herself; she was falling for him. Hard. Common sense told her it was a bad idea to get involved with someone you've only known for a week. He'd be leaving town once this case was solved, so wishful thinking was just that. Perhaps it would be better for both of them if they stayed friends. But that was how God worked, wasn't it? He brings you exactly what you need when you least expect it. Even things you didn't know you needed.

*God, we need to find Uncle Dan's killer.*

A pang of guilt hit her stomach. She was the do-it-yourself kind of person and that meant most times; she forgot to ask for God's help.

The computer monitor in front of her dimmed, indicating that it was about to power down. The flicker pulled her attention back to her work. Yes, getting her mind off the case was the best thing to do. She tapped the enter key to stop the sleep mode process. The article she'd worked on for the past hour reappeared. She needed to get it done and turned it in before anything else went wrong.

She set her fingers to work, forcing her mind to send words to her fingertips. The room echoed the clicking sound of each key she pressed.

The sound of a door closing flowed by footsteps grabbed her attention. It was probably her mom with lunch. Before she started typing again, she listened to the sound of footsteps. They were deep, meaning whoever was making them was wearing heavy shoes instead of the ballerina flats she'd let her mom borrow this morning.

Maybe it was Kyle. They'd had a break in the case and he came here to tell her in person. She stood and circled the desk. Her heart sped up slightly as she pictured his face. It was all she could do to keep the corners of her mouth from climbing to a smile.

She was halfway to the door when the knob turned. It opened. Her blood turned to ice when Victor stepped into the room with a switch's blade in his hand.

"What are you doing here?" She asked, knowing exactly why he was there.

"You ruined my life. I'm here to return the favor." He took a step toward her. She took a step back. Her mind raced, trying to come up with a way out of this. He was between her and the door. A weapon. She needed her handgun. It was in her purse behind the desk. Victor lunged at her, swinging the knife. She dove out of the way, falling to the floor on her back.

He came over and stood over her. He leaned down and grabbed her shoulder. She placed both feet in his stomach and pushed him off with all she had. He ended up on the floor a few feet away. Meg got up and half crawled toward the desk. If she could just get her handgun. There wasn't time to call for help. No one would hear her if she screamed.

She felt Victor's iron grip on her ankle and the violent tug as he tried to drag her across the floor. A searing pain shot through the back of her head like a lightning bolt, and everything went dark. He had hit her. And if she didn't do something fast, it would be too late. With every fiber of her being, she gathered herself up onto her hands and knees and began scrambling toward the desk, away from Victor's grasp. But it was too late; he struck her again with blinding force, sending her crashing to the floor. She knew then that this was her fate - just like Uncle

Dan. She was going to die in Victor's cold hands.

*****

Kyle really needed to take some time off to reconnect with his brother, once this case was solved, and maybe even get to know Meg a little better. He'd never met anyone like her. She was a spunky, kind-hearted ginger. He drew in a deep breath to counteract the tightness in his chest that picturing her smile brought. She was the only woman to actually take his breath away.

"I think we should do one more sweep of these woods to make sure we haven't missed anything," Michael said from the driver's seat. Shoot, how long had he been talking? He'd been so deep in thought about

Meg that he didn't hear anything before that. "I think that's a good idea," He replied, hoping he sounded as if he understood everything Michael said. At least what he heard made it easy for him to pretend that he had been listening.

"Are you going to answer my question?" Michael asked. Kyle opened his mouth to respond just as his phone started buzzing in his pocket. He pulled it out and tapped the button to answer it. Saved by the bell. Meg's name was across the screen.

"Hello?"

"Yes, is this Kyle the Private Investigator?"

"Yes, who is this?" He knew who it was by the sound of her voice but he didn't want to come across as weird.

"It's Megan's mother, Patricia. Please come to the Arbutus House as quickly as possible. Something is very wrong. I'm about to call the sheriff to have him meet us here as well,"

"He's here with me actually and we were on our way there to have another look around where your brother-in-law was found," He explained.

"I see. Please come to the main house first?" She said, her voice cracking as if she was about to cry or had already been crying.

"What's going on? Is Meg alright?" Why else would she call him from Meg's phone? He heard a sob come through the phone speaker.

"Please, just come quick," He heard a beep showing she'd hung up.

"Something's up. We need to get there now!" Kyle clenched his fists as Michael flipped on the siren and sped up.

*Lord, please let her be alright.*

His heart beat against his ribs. They reached the park in less than five minutes. It felt more like thirty to Kyle. He opened the door to climb out just as his brother brought the cruiser to a stop. Meg's mother came running up to them. Her face was red and swollen from crying.

"Tell us what happened, Mrs. Holmes," Michael commanded, circling the front of the car.

"She's gone! I went to get her lunch and came back, and she's gone!" She sobbed.

"She could've just gone to run an errand or something," Michael suggested, placing a comforting hand on her shoulder.

"No, she has an article due. She was supposed to answer the phone and take messages while she worked on it. She wouldn't have just taken off like that without telling me," she sobbed. Kyle could feel his heart speed up a little more with every word she said. He didn't want to fear the worst.

"Did she leave a note or anything?" He asked. Patricia shook her head.

"I looked for one, but all I found was this." She held up a small metal object in a trembling hand. It looked like an arrowhead with a handle on it. Judging by the T shape of the handle, the blade was meant to go between your fingers like Wolverine.

Michael's brow wrinkled as pulled a glove from his pocket and took the little weapon from her. Hopefully, they would find

Meg without needing to pull fingerprints from it.

"Where did you find that?"

"It was on the floor near the desk," Patricia's eyes widened. Michael's tone gave the impression that he'd seen it before.

"You've seen this before?" Kyle asked his brother.

"Simon Bradford has a forge behind his factory. He likes to make things like this. I'm pretty sure this is called a push dagger."

"A forge? You mean like making swords and knives and stuff?" He'd heard of metal workings making historically accurate weapons, but he'd never seen anything like this. Patricia wrung her hands.

"No way. Simon wouldn't do anything like this," she objected. Her gaze fell to the ground. Was she trying to convince herself that this Simon person wouldn't do this?

"Maybe not, but he'd know who else makes these. That'll at least give us something to go on,"

"Let's go then," Michael turned toward his police cruiser. Kyle took long strides to keep at his brother's heels. A loud gasp stopped them in their tracks and turned back toward Patricia.

"What is it?" Michael asked before Kyle finished forming the words. They both knew that every moment was critical and could instantly turn from a hostage rescue to body recovery.

"Meg covered the incident of the man found dead in Victor Bradford's apartment building last year. He came out here several times harassing her, claiming that she ruined his life," She explained.

"I remember that. He had to be escorted from the property," Michael added, stroking his stubble.

"Everyone moved out of his apartments and he eventually had to sell the place and move back in with his parents," Michael said to Kyle.

"So her article made him lose credibility in the eyes of the community," Yes. This had to be their guy.

"Yep. Don't worry, Mrs. Holmes. We'll find her," Michael said to Patricia, then continued to the car.

"Please bring my baby home safely," she called after them. She had to know they couldn't make any guarantees. Michael sped down the gravel road toward the main road, leaving Patricia with her face buried in her hands. Kyle wished more than anything that he could promise Meg would be home alive and well. But he was having trouble convincing himself of that.

# CHAPTER 7

Meg's head was like a ticking time bomb, ready to explode at any moment. The pain jabbed and pulsed at her temples like a needle puncturing skin. She tried to move, but it felt like she was encased in concrete, no matter how much she strained or struggled. Her vision was blurry at first, the world around her nothing more than a blur of indistinct shapes.

Gradually, clarity emerged through her foggy vision. She could make out where she was - tied up in an old wooden chair on a factory floor. The loud whining of machinery pierced through her skull like a drill boring through the rock, intensifying the pain. Slowly but surely, recognition dawned on her; this was the Bradford Metal factory. Victor Bradford came around the corner of a large grinding machine that seemed to be the loudest.

Meg's heart thumped against her rib cage as she looked around the room, her eyes darting from one corner to the next. She tried to take deep breaths and think logically, but panic had already settled in.

Victor slowly appears in front of her, a smug grin on his face.

"Look who's finally awake," he said, advancing closer toward her with each step.

Meg felt her heart pounding in her chest as panic flooded through her. She had to think of something, and fast. Sweat beaded on her forehead as she scrambled for words, desperately trying to buy time.

"I-I didn't mean it! I was only doing my job," she pleaded, her voice shaking.

Victor scoffed. "You knew exactly what you were doing. Your work for the newspaper has ruined more than one life in this town." His eyes burned dangerously, sending a chill of terror slithering down Meg's spine.

Meg's heart sank a little more with each step he took toward her. She was trapped. There was no telling what Victor had planned for her, but she knew it would result in her death.

As Victor leaned in closer, Meg could smell the scent of alcohol on his breath. He was clearly intoxicated and unstable. Meg's mind raced, trying to come up with a plan to escape. She strained against the ropes that bound her to the chair, but they didn't budge. She thought about trying to scream, but it wouldn't do any good with the loud machinery that surrounded her. At least if she was going to die, she could get some answers.

"Why did you kill Daniel Carroll? Why did you try to kill my mom?" She blurted out.

Victor's eyes narrowed and a dark, menacing aura surrounded him. Meg could sense the danger emanating from him.

"Because he was there with you when that man was killed at my apartment complex. He helped you with that story. The worse things got for me, the more I realized that both of you had destroyed my life. He was easy to take out. You, on the other hand, were a challenge. Just when I thought I had you, it turned out to be your mom. It's hard to tell you apart from behind,"

Her mom nearly lost her life because of Meg. They were both wearing green tops that day.

Meg gritted her teeth, disgusted with herself for being the reason her mother was almost killed. She couldn't let Victor get away with this. She had to stay calm and find a way out of this situation.

"You're sick, Victor. Killing innocent people won't bring back anything you lost," she said, trying to reason with him.

Victor let out a cold laugh. "Maybe not. But I can keep you from messing up someone else's life with your nosey 'job'".

Meg's heart raced as Victor reached into his pocket and pulled out a small switchblade. The glint of the metal caught her eye, and she swallowed hard, bracing herself for the worst. This was it. She had seconds left to live.

*****

Kyle's nerves were at a point where he felt sick to his stomach. What if they were already too late? He'd never forgive himself.

"I'm having another officer meet us there. It'll take some time to get a team together. Time we don't have,"

"Who is it?" Hopefully, it wasn't Clay. They didn't need someone who was out to get them. They needed someone they could trust to help rescue Meg.

"One of my best friends. Harry Miller,"

Michael's tone was steady, but Kyle could detect a sense of urgency in his brother's voice. He knew that if he trusted him, then Harry must be a good guy. Someone who they could trust to have their backs.

The car came to a sudden halt as they arrived at the Bradford Metal factory. Kyle's heart pounded in his chest as he looked around, trying to spot any sign of Meg. A few seconds later, another car came to a stop next to them. Michael's reaction told him that this was Harry.

They each had their guns out as they made their way toward the factory, Kyle's mind raced with all the possible scenarios that could be playing out inside. He hoped and prayed Meg was still alive, that they weren't too late.

The sound of machinery whirring filled the air, growing louder as they approached the entrance to the factory. Michael motioned for Kyle to stay back as they cautiously made their way inside.

He expected to find workers inside, but there was no one around. Was it some holiday or something? The huge empty building gave him a creepy vibe.

They crept through the factory, guns at the ready, Kyle's heart pounding with each step. The sound of machinery grew louder and more oppressive as they approached a large grinding machine. A chill ran down Kyle's spine as he imagined Meg tied up somewhere nearby, the grinding machine drowning out her screams for help.

As they rounded the corner to the back of the building. Meg was tied to a chair and nodded her head to the right. Victor must've heard them coming.

"He's making a run for it!" Kyle shouted, darting in the direction Meg was pointing toward.

Kyle glanced back to see Michael untying Meg. She was in good hands. He could fully focus on catching Victor. Harry was at his heels.

They could hear Victor's footsteps echoing through the factory as they chased after him. Kyle's heart pounded with adrenaline as they turned a corner and saw Victor disappearing through a door at the end of the hallway.

Kyle and Harry raced after him, guns drawn, ready for anything. They burst through the door and found themselves in a small room filled with machinery. Victor was in the process of climbing it and reaching toward a window. Harry stepped in front of

Kyle and reached for his ankle. Victor reach into his pocket and pulled something out, then threw it at Harry. He fell back, letting out a growl.

"Stop right there, Victor!" Kyle shouted, his voice echoing off the walls. He needed to check on Harry, but he couldn't let Victor get away, either.

He couldn't kill him, but he needed to stop him. He took aim and squeezed the trigger. Victor let out a scream as he fell back off the machine.

Kyle rushed over to Harry, who was lying on the ground, his hand covering the side of his face and neck. The handle of another push dagger was under his hand.

"Harry, are you okay?" Kyle asked, concern lacing his voice.

"I don't know," Harry groaned, gritting his teeth as he tried to sit up.

Kyle helped him to his feet, and they both made their way over to where Victor lay, groaning in pain. Kyle knelt beside him and checked his pulse. It was weak, but he was still alive.

Michael and Meg appeared in the doorway. Kyle went to her, and Michael dropped down next to his friend.

"We heard the sirens a moment ago. Help is almost here." Harry gave Michael a firm pat on the shoulder. As if thanking him. It was probably best that he did that, because talking would make him lose blood faster.

Several EMTs and Police officers burst into the room. The scene was secured, and the wounded were whisked off on gurneys.

Kyle couldn't help but think about what had just happened. Meg was safe, and Victor was going to face justice for what he had done. But the events of the past few days had taken a toll on him, and he knew that it would take time for him to recover. He had come close to losing the girl he'd fallen for.

He pushed any what-ifs out of his mind. The case was closed. Meg was safe, and she kept his promise to her.

With a deep breath, Kyle turned to Meg and took her hand in his. "Are you okay?" he asked, his voice soft and gentle.

She nodded, tears welling up in her eyes. "I'm okay. Thanks to you."

Kyle pulled her into a tight embrace, holding her close. He never wanted to let her go. It was as if he was holding onto life itself. Yes, feeling this way about a woman he'd met a few days ago was sudden. But he knew in his heart that it was meant to be.

# CHAPTER 8

## One Month Later,

Meg drew in a deep breath of the sweet fragrance that laced the morning air around the Arbutus House. She was standing on the porch, taking in the view of the beautiful flower garden that surrounded the house. It was peaceful and calm, a stark contrast to the chaos and danger of what took place here a few weeks ago. Meg couldn't help but feel grateful for Kyle. He had saved her life and had been there for her every step of the way.

She felt safe with him, like nothing could harm her as long as he was by her side.

He'd come to mean so much to her in such a short time. As if on cue, Kyle appeared on the porch, carrying two cups of steaming coffee. He handed her one and leaned against the railing, taking a sip from his cup.

"I've never watched a Civil War reenactment before,"
He said, glancing out at the grounds. "It's hard to imagine a battle being fought in such a peaceful place."
Meg nodded in agreement. "It's strange how history can change a place so much."

"I got a call about another case," The statement seemed to come out of nowhere. This was the very thing she'd tried to prepare her heart for this past month. He would leave Oakwood Springs.

"I'm not going to take it though,"

"You're not?"

"Nope, I want to be here when my niece or nephew is born. I want to be a good uncle."

"You will be," She smiled at him.

"I also want to get the nerve to ask you out,"

Kyle's words hung in the air, causing Meg's heart to skip a beat. She had been hoping he would say something like that, but she was also nervous. Before Meg could respond, Kyle took a step closer to her, his eyes searching hers.

"I know we've only known each other for a short time, but I feel like we have a connection that's hard to ignore. I want to explore that connection with you, if you're willing."

Meg's heart swelled with emotion as she looked into Kyle's deep, soulful eyes. She had never felt this way about anyone before, and she knew that she wanted to take a chance on him.

"I would like that," she said, a smile spreading across her face. "I would really like that."

Kyle's face lit up with a grin, and he leaned in to kiss her. The kiss was gentle at first, but quickly deepened into something more. Meg melted into his embrace, feeling like she was exactly where she was meant to be.

As they pulled away from each other, Kyle took her hand in his. "So, what do you say we go explore this town together? Maybe grab some lunch and see where the day takes us?"

Meg grinned, feeling a sense of excitement bubbling up inside of her. "I'd like that," she said, feeling like the future was full of endless possibilities as long as she was with Kyle.

# THE END

# AUTHOR'S NOTE

Hello Readers,

I'm so happy you decided that you were up for another adventure in Oakwood Springs. As you may have noticed, this story isn't as long as Fury in the Shadows. The reason for that is because I've spent a lot of time in prayer over this series. I was sure where I was going to take it, but God had something else in mind. He kept bringing me the story of the Prodigal Son. Michael and Kyle are brothers whose lives turned out very different from one another. Kyle felt like a failure, always living in the shadow of his big brother. But his view of himself kept him from seeing that his family still cared about him no matter what.

You probably noticed that in this retelling of the story, Michael fits more into the role of the Prodigals father than his brother. I feel that God wanted me to write the story this way to serve as a reminder of the scripture in Luke 6 where Jesus tells us to do unto others as we would have them do unto us.

I hope this word encourages you and feeds your soul. I am so thankful for each of you and hope you continue reading my books and supporting my work.

Happy Reading!

# ABOUT THE AUTHOR

**Rebecca Hemlock** is an Award-winning author and has written articles, books, and short stories for many years. She has worked as a freelance journalist for 4 years. She is currently a member of Sisters in Crime and American Christian Fiction Writers. Her books have also made it to the Amazon.com #1 bestseller list several times.

Aside from writing Romance and suspense, Rebecca enjoys writing children's fiction. Her first children's book, The Lost Soldier, was published in 2016 by Westbow Press. She has a total of 3 children's books, all published under the name R.C. Burch from 2016 to 2017. Rebecca has earned a degree in English and an Appalachian Studies certificate in Creative Writing. Her favorite times to write are early in the morning when the sun is coming up and at sunset. Rebecca lives in Eastern Kentucky with her husband and children

She could hear her pulse beating in her ears. The woods were farther away than they looked. Still, she wasn't about to let this person get away. She'd run twenty miles if she had to. It made no sense why anyone would want to kill Scott. For as long as she could remember, he'd taken the role of a father figure in her life.

Kelly sprinted to keep up with her partner. If only she had Sandy here. She'd let her off the leash. Chip was more than eager to do the job, but he was still new and could be unpredictable. She wasn't sure she trusted him yet, despite being hopeful that he would do well today. Mentally calculating, it told her that the woods were about a quarter of a mile away. Sandy wouldn't have been able to make a run like this.

Kelly pushed the image of her retired police dog napping in her living room out of her mind when they entered the edge of the woods. A black figure about forty yards ahead of her leaped over a fallen tree before he zipped to the left and disappeared. Chip's eyes were locked in that direction, occasionally dipping his head to smell the ground, ensuring that he was taking her the right way. It would take a miracle for her to catch up to the shooter, but she would keep following Chip as long as he had the scent. He sped up. Maybe he was closer than she thought. Her lungs began to burn. She had to take this guy down. She would get justice for her brother. Chip stopped out of nowhere. His attention was drawn to their left. She'd seen the shooter turn to the right up ahead. So what could've gotten his attention? He stood motionless. His ears twitched. Had he lost the trail? There was no way.

SIGN UP FOR REBECCA'S NEWSLETTER
AND KEEP UP TO DATE ON BOOK
RELEASES AND EVENTS AT

# REBECCAHEMLOCK.COM